Going Out With Peacocks

and Other Poems

BOOKS BY URSULA K. LE GUIN

NOVELS
Tehanu
Always Coming Home
The Eye of the Heron
The Beginning Place
Malafrena
Very Far Away from Anywhere Else
The Word for World Is Forest
The Dispossessed
The Lathe of Heaven
The Farthest Shore
The Tombs of Atuan
A Wizard of Earthsea
The Left Hand of Darkness
City of Illusions
Planet of Exile
Rocannon's World

SHORT STORIES
Searoad
Buffalo Gals
The Compass Rose
Orsinian Tales
The Wind's Twelve Quarters

FOR CHILDREN
Fish Soup • *A Ride on the Red Mare's Back*
Catwings Return • *Catwings*
Fire and Stone
A Visit from Dr. Katz
Leese Webster

POETRY AND CRITICISM
Dancing at the Edge of the World
Wild Oats and Fireweed
Hard Words
The Language of the Night
Wild Angels

Going Out With Peacocks

and Other Poems

URSULA K. LE GUIN

HarperPerennial
A Division of HarperCollinsPublishers

HarperCollins books may be purchased for educational, business, or sales promotional use. For information please write: Special Markets Department, HarperCollins Publishers, Inc., 10 East 53rd Street, New York, NY 10022.

FIRST EDITION

Designed by Alma Hochhauser Orenstein

Library of Congress Cataloging-in-Publication Data

Le Guin, Ursula K., 1929–
    Going out with peacocks and other poems / by Ursula K. Le Guin.—1st ed.
       p. cm
    ISBN 0-06-055356-1/ISBN 0-06-095057-9 (pbk.)
    I. Title.
PS3562. E42G65   1994   93-43624
811'.54—dc20

---

94 95 96 97 98 ❖/RRD 10 9 8 7 6 5 4 3 2 1

94 95 96 97 98 ❖/RRD 10 9 8 7 6 5 4 3 2 1 (pbk.)

Acknowledgments

The following poems first appeared in:

"Ariadne Dreams": *Star Line,* 1989
"Keeping Rocks": *Whale Song,* 1990
"Riding the 'Coast Starlight'": *Amicus Journal,* 1991
"The Pacific Slope," "Praying to Ecola Creek," "Mouth of the Kla-
     math," "Sun Setting at Cannon Beach," "My Music," "Getting
     On": *Calapooya Collage,* 1991, 1992
"Marilyn" and "Buzzard Visit": *Mr. Cogito,* 1993
"The Queen of Spain": *Cream City Review,* 1993
"Sunt lacrimae rerum" and "The Red Dancers": *Prairie Schooner,* 1993
"Semen" and "To the Next Guests": *Hubbub,* 1993
"Three McKenzie River Poems": *Rain City Review,* 1993
"Werewomen" and "For Judith": *UrbanUS,* 1993
"Fragments from the Women's Writing": *Beloit Poetry Journal,* 1992,
     and *Full Spectrum Four,* 1993
"A True Story" and "The Book to Have": *The Burnside Reader,* 1993
"Dreaming California" and "Waking: Two Poems": *International
     Dream Quarterly,* 1993
"The Woman and the Soul": *Thirteenth Moon,* 1993
"A Discourse on Method": *Northwest Review,* 1993
"The Years," "Looking for Proxy Falls," "Gulls Puddling: January,"
     "In the Siskiyous in May": *The Cafe Review,* 1994
"In That Desert": *The American Voice,* 1994

"Phoenicians" was printed as a broadside by Press-22 with an illus-
     tration by Henk Pander, 1984

"The Vigil for Ben Linder" was printed as a broadside for the
     Women's International League for Peace and Freedom, 1987

Contents

FOUR • Dancing on the Sun

ᐁ One ᐁ

FIRE, WATER, EARTH, BREATH

Three McKenzie River Poems

LAST OF AUGUST

In what meter does the wind blow on a river?
Can I know the clear feet of the water?
An older measure, longer yet suddener.
Boulders under the bright flood mutter
of the mountains, imitating thunder.
A dead tree on the other shore falls in one slow
    drumbeat.

CABIN 4, CEDARWOOD LODGE

Leaves lie and lower in the air, yellow,
and flutter to the water to vanish.
Dry alders full of amber sunlight
stir, and the cottonwoods flicker
under the osprey's remembered,
heavy, silent flying. Why am I heavy,
so dry of heart, so silent?
Where are my people? Do I cast a shadow?
Am I banished from the spring?
If I'm falling, let me cry aloud.
If I fly, let me know my wings.

I turn, and all the trees are massed
in the reflecting glass door, yellow-green
against black vacancy, stirring and trembling,
and the river races through its own echoes.

⤳

How low sun strikes green streambank,
dark tree trunks, moss-blurred rocks, ferns,
in a gleam of sweet detail
across the incessant river-movement:
it matters. As I write the word,
a young squirrel runs across the deck, thin,
delicate, intent on something
directly before it, large eyes staring,
soft tail following, confirming
that it matters.
Now the light's cloudier
and the bushes agitated, tossing
their arms, and the screen door
yawns creaking open and bangs
again, and the river
is as it must be incessant,
merciless, disinterested.

DROUTH

Many people have put their heads up out of the river
to look at the year with no rain.
They have tufts of dry hair
and look surprised, but peaceful.

March in Beloit

Black branches of big oaks
complicate the bells
clanking on the cold wind. Snow
lies on the north side
of every rock and morning.
Empty earthmounds
of the older powers
hide winter in them,
but a cardinal calls fire!
from bare labyrinths, and the bells strike
always an hour other than the hour.

The Pacific Slope

I love that, "the Pacific Slope," I see
snowtiger cloudy granite of the Sierras
and silver scree of the Cascades, vast sweeps
and westward slidings down to wild oats and oaks
in valleys, cresting to the Coast Range then
tangled in ceanothus and salal, and last
fast falling off cliff, down dune, slopes
sweet in fog and sunlight to the sea.

In the Siskiyous in May

The eastern mountain's shadow
lies on the western mountain.

The red-armed madrone
all day holds up a crown
of tiny ivory urns to the sun.

The western mountain's shadow
lies on the eastern mountain.

Moonlight lies easy
all over the mountains
on the crowns of the madrones.

Keeping Rocks

Rocks hold down my flying
papers, my worktable,
my house. I hold me down
with the rocks I put in my pockets.
I keep away from rivers.
Weighty little chunks
of my country
hold me to it
ever more nearly.

Looking for Proxy Falls

for Monza

No falls.
Only a climbing
lightly through forests
till the five white peaks rise
out of torment of black lava to the sky
and a laughing come-down
past the absent sign
silently hiding
what falls.

Consider

Industrious and diligent, the lily
toils to spin its white shirt
out of dirt, light, and water.
A wise field-worker,
it fools the Bible.

Sleeping with Cats

In smoothness of darkness are
warm lumps of silence.
There are no species.
Purring recurs.

From Lorenzo

I feel that barred and mottled tabby
coat of fur fits me,
it's my claws fixed in that crabapple tree
and my gasoline green glare
on the bird above me.
My wings bear me from the bough
so lightly, and I feel
the bark and tender cambium
under it and my leaves playing
with the wind. I climb myself
and fly away.

Gulls Puddling: January

All down the thundering, freezing beach
seagulls stand just above the breakers
working their thin legs very quickly
back and forth and back and forth
like cats covering cat shit.
Thus they make little basins in the sand
from which they snap up two or three
somethings and eat them.
They walk away then
with the disinterested expression of gulls,
leaving perfectly circular soupbowls
of bitter water down the beach
till the next wave.

The two-faced god of winter
watches yet always looks away.

Buzzard Visit

It came on the sound its fingerfeathers
make the air make,
but it was silent. Was a silence. Folded
up its great hands
that hold winds,
settled its feet on a dead elm branch
firmly, cocked
that narrow, blood-colored head
like a pistol barrel
at me, underneath. I am not dead,
yet, I said, but it waited
to see what I was doing.
Look, I said, I'm sewing!
But it knew we're all, whatever else
we may be doing, dying.
The head was so fitted to red holes
and the beak to making them
as to be frightening,
but it was a patient, curious,
maybe a cheerful,
(within the windsound
of the wide dark wings)
even a restful, silence.

Praying to Ecola Creek

for Joy Johannessen

Allow me the little netted waves
in the sunlight, the little shallow
clear watershadows, rectangles,
fishscales, and movements constantly
trembling and returning and vanishing,
allow me the shallow creek running
into the sea and the long low small
waves running inland to meet it,
allow this clarity to my spirit
to be sunlit and transparent
and constantly going out and coming in
and meeting itself and the other quietly.

Mouth of the Klamath

The mouth of the river
sucks at the springs in the mountains.
It is her thighs that open here
wide among sandbars to the sea.
She lies down long, the river, and her salmon
swim up in her and breeding die, and she
gives herself and all her children to the sea,
the sea that lies down long and wide
to nurse the sky with rainy milk
that the mountains are sucking
from the soft breasts of the fog.

Sun Setting at Cannon Beach

It makes this loud noise.
This great light shines.
That old tree stands to break the light in two.
I need a new tongue.

My old tongue breaks in two
knowing the left word and the right word
but not the loud word of ocean
or the great light word.

TWO

FURY AND SORROW

Riding the "Coast Starlight"

I saw white pelicans rise
from the waters of morning
in the wide valley, going.
I saw trees white with snow
rise silent from clouds
in the deep mountains, returning.
Heavy, noble, solemn the gesture
of the wings, the branches,
a white writing on destruction.

Processing Words

I want to dream out words of anger
on this machine that states my mind
in this late summer night that leans to fall.

Kind and stately buildings lean to fall,
the Libraries, the Public Schools; the dream
of a republic of the mind is undermined.

The hunger of poverty is hunger,
the hunger of satiety is anger.
The state of war is a machine

that holds a lien on minds and words.
The kind republic that we dreamed
of building falls to night.

Marilyn

Why is she so, the poor sweet bird,
the bird so caged, that sang
out of all nature to the Emperor?
Had she no right to age?

Did you wind her up too tight?

I only want, you said, my toy
of rosy gold, the sweet bulbul
in silky panties gold and red
and ivory forever young and moist and vulnerable; but, my boy, she's dead.
A bit of bone, a bit of mould.

Cover the cage, good night, good night.

In That Desert

written for the AIDS Wall in Portland, 1989

A lizard with no tail
looked at me and its flicked tongue
said: Belief in punishment
is punishment, belief
in sin is sin.

Its eye like a black stone
said: Love is punished
terribly. Belief
is a dry torrent.
The fire I die in
flickers my bright wings.

The Hands of Torturers

They hold the hoses, flip the switches,
grip and beat and cut the bodies, then
unzip and tend to their own hose pissing,
tuck it back in, run the razor
tender down the cheekbone, chuck
a buttock, fondle breasts, part labia.
From one body to another
how easily the hands can go.

Werewomen

I want to go moonwalking
on it or under it I don't care
I just want to go moonwalking
alone.
   Women in their sixties
don't go to the moon,
   women in the cities
don't go out alone.
   But I want O listen what I want
is to be not afraid.
Listen what I need is freedom.
   Women in their sixties
think about dying,
   women in the cities
think about dying,
   all kinds of women
think about lying,
think about lying alone.
   But listen there's a moon out there
and I don't want sex and I don't want death
and I don't want what you think I want
only to be a free woman.
   What is that, a free woman,
   a young free woman,

an old free woman?
   Asking for the moon.
Women in their sixties
   have no moon.
Women in the cities
   howl at the moon.
All kinds of women
talk about walking alone.
When the moon is full
listen how they howl,
listen how they howl together.

Cry No More

U.S. Surgeon General Antonia Novello has estimated that every five years domestic violence claims 58,000 lives in the United States—as many as were lost in the Vietnam War.
—*The Oregonian,* February 20, 1992

There's a long black wall
and people walk along the grass
and touch the names and cry.

There's a wall of wind.
You can't see the names
carved in it, you can't see the wall,
you can't even cry.

Tell me her name.

Tell me her name and I will build a wall
of the names of the dead
killed in the long war,
and the wall will go around the world
like a wind, like a long wind blowing,
blowing, blowing.

Touch the names,
tell the names,
say the names
and cry: No more!

Her Silent Daughter

For Tawana Brawley

They have this statue: Justice.
This blindfold woman, I don't know
what woman, she's good-looking
but she's not Justice. Justice
is a man. Plugs in his ears.
Maybe they're hearing aids.
He weighs what he wants with what he gets
in these scales he made. Justice
tunes in on some men OK but has never heard
one woman say one word.

So this statue doesn't see this woman.
She is fifteen and she is written
foul names on and cut and rubbed
with dog shit and stuffed
into a plastic garbage bag
and the man says, "Why did you do this
to yourself?" to her.
He says, "Explain to us what happened,"
to her.
He says, "Why don't you answer?

What have you got to fear?"
to her.

My statue, I have a statue, is a woman
blind with tears. She keeps looking all over
    the world
for her daughter that was taken from her,
her silent daughter
that the king of shit and money
took to the garbage kingdom
for his use forever.

Until she finds her
it will be winter.

Sentence

Freedom of speech being protected by the First
Amendment,
there is no problem, because there is no evil, only
behavior, so that I approve of what he says,
since disapproval would be like some prude or
   fundamentalist
politician of whom I disapprove of course,
and will defend his right to say it
because, free speech being a fundamental right,
   the rights
of the little boys and little girls used
by him to make his pornographic
statements and the little women
snuffed by him to make his snuff
statements (which are of course protected
by the First Amendment) are no problem,
since the little children and the little women
who make his statements for him
by laying their unprotected
bodies on, as it were, the line,
the bottom line, say nothing,

and so have no speech to be protected
by the First Amendment, and so there is no evil,
but only the pursuit of happiness and the rights
of man, which are, of course,
fundamental.

Phoenicians

We lived forever until 1945.

Children have time to make mistakes,
margin for error. Carthage
could be destroyed and sown with salt.
Everything was always. It would be all right.

Then we turned
(so technically sweet the turning)
the light on.
And in the desert of that dividing light
we saw the writing on the walls of the world.

Birds can't read it. It blinds them.
They blunder in the air and fall
like feather cinders.
Fetus of sheep and woman and dolphin,
spawn of salmon, seed of alder,
wordless in shadow:
dark is the blessing on them,
darkness, and silence, and water.

But we literate, grown mortal,
have no time to turn again
and must turn again,
have no room to turn round
and must turn round
to read the words through to the end
aloud with mouths of salt and tongues of sand,
learning to ask blessing of what dies.

Hiroshima! O City of the Light!
May light's dead center at the last
be the eggshell broken,
may the bird reborn arise,
soft-winged, dark feather-plumed,
heavy among earth's shadows,
the word spoken by the waters.

The Vigil for Ben Linder

killed in 1986 by "contras" while working as an engineer in
a volunteer group bringing electric power to villages in
Nicaragua

This rain among the candle flames
under the heavy
end of April evening
falls so softly on us
listening
that it dissolves us
like salt.

A child frets.
The grieving over names.
The same anger.
There are still far countries.

Mayday! they signal,
it's sinking, crashing, it's going
down now! Mayday!
But it used to mean
you went into the garden
early, that first morning,
to make a posy

for a neighbor's door,
or boldly offered —
"These are for your daughter!" —
laughing, because she wasn't up yet.
They were maybe twelve years old.
Afterwards
they went to different schools.

The bringing of light
is no simple matter.
The offering of flowers
is a work of generations.

Young men are scattered
like salt on a dry ground.
Not theirs, not theirs,
but ours
the brave children
who must learn the rules.

To bring light
to flower in a dark country
takes experts in illumination,
engineers of radiance.

Taken, taken and broken.

We are dim circles flickering
at nightfall in April in the rain

that quickens the odor of flowering trees
and the odor of stone.
Over us
is a dark government.

Circles of burning flames, of flowers,
of children learning light.
Circles of rain on stone and skin.
Turning and returning in shaken silence,
broken, unbroken.
Sorrow is the home country.

Fragments from the Women's Writing

In the 1980s, a Chinese linguist discovered a group of elderly women in Hunan who used an ancient script, written and read exclusively by women, which "uses an inverted system of grammar and syntax very different from Chinese." The writing resembles oracle bone carvings from the Shang dynasty (sixteenth century B.C.) and writing of the Chin dynasty (third century B.C.). Local women believe the script, which mothers taught their daughters at home, was invented by a Song dynasty concubine to relieve her loneliness, but Professor Gong Zhibing thinks the language, too complex to be the creation of one person, is a relic of writing systems lost when Chinshi Huangdi, the First Emperor, united China in 221 B.C. Chinshi Huangdi unified Chinese writing by forbidding the use of all scripts except his official "small seal" characters. Men learned the new official writing. Women, barred from schools, kept the old script alive in private.

Most of the writing is poetry, autobiography, letters, and songs. Girls would form sworn-sister relationships, "using the script to document their bonds and correspond with one another long after they were grown and married. Few of the writings have survived, because the women asked that all their writings be burned when they died, so that they could read their favorite works in the afterlife." Professor Gong met two women in their eighties still able to read and write the language. The only surviving members of a seven-member sworn-sister "family," the two had burned all the copies of a third sister's writings when she died.

I read the information above in a clipping from *The China Daily* of Beijing, and wrote the following imaginary translations in 1992. Since then I have seen a publisher's announcement of genuine translations of the women's writing.

Fragments from the Women's Writing

Daughter: these are the characters
forbidden by the Emperor.
These are the bone words,
the cracks on the under-shell.
This is the other grammar.

⁓

Sister: I document our bond
and correspond to you
finger to finger, eye to eye.

⁓

Unwrap the old silk very slowly.

⁓

Daughter: write in milk,
as I did. Hold it to the fire
to make the words appear.

⁓

Sister: still my sleeves are dry,
but I saw a dark moon this autumn
a long way down the river.

My Lord was angry till I told him
it was my laundry list.
He laughed then, "Hen scratchings!"
and I laughed.

Daughter: learn the language upside down,
inverted in the turtle's eye.
Use the bones for soup.

An army of men
of heavy red pottery
under the hill by the river
where we do the laundry.

Sister: His thighs are jade
and his staff a stiff bamboo,
but there's nobody here to talk to.

Do not burn all your songs, mother,
much as you may love them.
How can I sing smoke?
Leave me the one about autumn.

Sister: This form is my own.
I live inside these words
as the turtle in its shell,
as the marrow in the bone.

‏‏‎ ‎⸕

Sisters: This is a colder mountain
than the tiger's, and the bones
say only snow is falling.

⸕

Daughters: Keep my embroideries,
send my life after me.
My autobiography was the turtle's under-shell,
the small cracks in bones,
a silken thread, a drop of milk.
A life too vast
for the little writing of the Emperor.

⸕

I crack each word of your letter
and suck its sweetness.
How it will sing in the fire!

⸕

Sisters: Burn me, burn me,
let the snow fall in the river!

⸕

Mother: I entered college as a man
but they exposed my body
and wrote their small words on it
till it shrank to shadow.
I put on the turtle's shell
and crawled into the fire.
In the cracked oracle
you can read that the Empire
will fall.

↝

Our characters
have always been forbidden.
Will the last daughters
unroll the silk kept secret
through all the dynasties,
or turn our words to fire?

↝

Sister: I am lonely. Write.

Three

KIN AND KIND

A True Story

for John Henley

My friend got Vachel Lindsay into her computer
and couldn't get him out. He'd hide but not delete.
She'd be bringing up a spreadsheet
and up would come the Congo, gold and black,
or in the middle of a catalog of rare editions
there'd be General Booth entering heaven
and the drums beating, or that prairie bird singing
sweet — sweet — sweet —

Try WordPerfect, people said, try Microsoft Word.
But she was afraid
she might get Whitman, maybe even Milton.
She guessed she'd stay with Vachel
and the prairie bird.

The Book to Have

I have a friend who's
going to have
this book.
    It is a good book.
    It is a true book.
It tells my friend
who,
it tells her who her grandmother
was it tells her
who her mother
was it tells her
who her daughter is
it tells.
    It is the good book.
    It is the true book.
Even it tells her
that her daddy
did. It tells
her that even
he did that. It
tells her even
that. He did.
    And even so it is
    a good, true book.

It tells my friend
who I am, who
her friend is, tells
her her friend is who
she is. It tells her
who she is.
   She says she will have it
   real soon now.

Dreaming California

for Charles

A great oval opened in the dream sky,
full of perfectly ordinary people
with musical instruments, not playing them.
I called you to come out on the porch and see.
The oval closed, and behind St. John Mountain
which was higher than itself
we saw another mountain
still higher, and then behind it
higher and higher in the sunlit mist
more mountains going up, and up, and up.
Then the bell tower of a cathedral
between us and the mountains
was standing vastly tall and misty.
We said, It must be an image,
a mirage reflecting
some real tower somewhere.
We went to tell the others in the kitchen
because it made us so happy,
the sunlight, the mountains, the tower.
When we all came out on the porch
the fog had come in low and wet
and silent, and that was all we saw.

For Judith

"... and this word
bumping around in the landscape ..."

—JUDITH BARRINGTON

But it's a soft word, Judith!
If you said a word for its softness,
you might say *billowy,*
or *valley floor,* or *lesbian.*
If you made up an unbumpy sound,
you might come out with *ahloovay,*
or *elyamoor,* or *lesbian.*
The ell, the zz, the buh, the nn —
how could you make a kinder noise?
Or say *The Isle of Lesbos:*
soft hills above a purple sea,
a wind sound, a shell murmur,
even to one who inhabits
one of the right-angled landscapes.
Exile is also a soft word.

The Years

The years come all colors
like the rags
in the rag-basket my great-aunt
made her round rugs from,
circling the strips of calico,
polkadot, roman stripe, solid and paisley
round one another, braided
together, so that I walk on them
sixty years later,
those circles of faded colors.

The Woman and the Soul

There was a woman kept a soul
in a box, all folded up
like a paper doll, and she'd take it out
and put the paper clothes on it
and fold the little paper tabs
to hold the clothes onto the soul.
Party clothes for parties
Shopping clothes for shopping
Wedding dress for wedding
Swimming suit for swimming
Sexy suit for sex.
Afterwards
she'd take off the clothes and fold them
and fold the soul and put it in the box.

After the wedding she discovered
that he had a box too,
that he kept out in the garage.
She never saw him open it.
When the kids were grown she asked him once,
but he said he'd lost the key.
Mine never had a key, she said.
She'd been so busy with people and things
she hadn't thought about the box

for years. She found it in the attic
and opened it and took out the soul.

It had outgrown the clothes.
It had been growing in the attic
in the dark, it was pale
but it looked all right.
After a while it came downstairs
and lived in her closet with her clothes,
coming out sometimes
in the very early morning
to have breakfast with her.
And they talked.

When her husband died
she buried his box in the coffin with him
unopened and without a key.
The children came for the funeral
and the soul left the closet
and followed them around,
and they patted it and said, Good soul!
and went away again.
So she talked to it.
And it kept growing,
filling up all the rooms.
There she was in the house alone
with this huge soul.
It didn't fit.
It bulged out the windows.

One morning early
she opened all the doors
and the soul came outside.
Follow me, she said,
and went down to the beach.
Go on! she said when they were on the beach,
Go on!
And the soul got as large as the sky,
like the rain clouds,
and ran across the sea with the south wind,
and went up with the mountains and down with
    the rain.
How can I keep you now? she said.

Don't worry,
said the soul.
It's my turn.
And it put her gently in the box
with all her pretty clothes
and kept her.

The Queen of Spain, Grown Old and Mad, Writes to the Daughter She Imagines She Had by Christopher Columbus

Most beautiful,
I disclaim you.
You are not my new found land
nor my Hesperides
nor my America.
You are not mine
and I do not name you.
  I tear up the map
of the world of you
that had your rivers
in the wrong places,
imaginary mountains,
false passes leading my expeditions
to quicksands,
cannibals, jaguars.
  Most truthful,
I disown you:
I do not own you.
Truly, I have never known you.
  When you tell me
who you are
I will call you by that name.

When you tell me
where you are
my compass will point there.
When you tell me
of your prairies, your sierras,
I will see them in the blue air
above the western sea.
    O golden Peru,
treasure never mine,
most beautiful, most true!
Between us
is neither forgiveness
nor reparation
but only the sea waves, the sea wind.
    If ever you send
across the sea,
bells will be rung
in the old towers
and the Te Deum sung.
Crowned, jeweled, furred,
I will come forward:
Tell me, my Lord Ambassadors!
from the New World
what word, what word?

My Hero

for Caroline

Hesitant, frozen by the face
reflected in her shiny borrowed shield,
my hero stands —

and does she drop the sword?
Does she behead herself?

No. There are better things to do
with anger, with beauty,
with a headful of serpents
who can hiss wisdom; there must

be a story for my dear young hero.

It will not be the old story.

Puye: An Anasazi Village

for Elisabeth

The place said
I am the woman
I am to become.

The place found me
before you found it
in the long early
morning golden light
and the place said
my name
the place said my name
is Puye
and my name that was
is not known now.
I am the old one
the woman your daughter
who is to become
who is to be
beloved
and the woman who finds me
names me.

Concerning Theo

If I tried to imagine
the son I didn't have
if I hadn't had one,
I could never ever imagine
the one I did have.
The beauty of him!
His big nose!
His voice with its dry edge
in which the fifteen-year-old's still hiding
along with some sexy man of fifty,
oh, a voice to melt answering machines.
And he is so kind and so funny!
And he never sits down!
And he flies to Jakarta!
Never could I imagine
such a person. Not in my wildest.
When he was three
he would fling his arms
about me at knee level
thus rendering me immobile
and cry in his then very sweet
high voice, "Mama!
Don't *wowwy* bout it!"
OK, OK. I won't
worry about it.

Song for Caroline

Near can be turned to far,
Sea can be turned to land.
You will not turn from what you are
   For any man.

Where your heart goes, go,
Where your soul is, stand.
Do not be moved from what you know
   By any man.

Song for Elisabeth

Mother of my granddaughter,
Listen to my song:
A mother can't do right,
A daughter can't be wrong.

I have no claim whatever
On amnesty from you;
Nor will she forgive you
For anything you do.

So are we knit together
By force of opposites,
The daughter that unravels
The skein the mother knits.

One must be divided
So that one be whole,
And this is the duplicity
Alleged of woman's soul.

To be that heavy mother
Who weighs in every thing
Is to be the daughter
Whose footstep is the Spring.

Granddaughter of my mother,
Listen to my song:
Nothing you do will ever be right,
Nothing you do is wrong.

Four

DANCING ON THE SUN

Going Out With Peacocks

She leans to spring   the jaguar
the merciless year

My will is with decorum
a becoming peace

Against the will to stake all
on a stammered word

filch dregs from the table
I set and served

as hawk stoop   rabbit
scream   dying

woman   drunk driving
the jaguar car

Bale's Mill in the Napa Valley

Everything was always
grist to my mill,

the high redwood wheel
groaning and turning in the splash and spray
of water shooting from the sluice,
the slow gears
unlocked, the two stones
that never touch, the terrible weight
poised like a hoverfly
over the corn, beginning to turn,
and the coarse gold pouring
sweet and dry into the hand,
into the sacks
that were carried away.

The creek runs in its own course.
The stone lies on the stone.
The wheel stands still.
The grain stands
cut or uncut, sacred
in unending fields,
wild oats on the shaken hills.

The wheel of the summer night
turns, and the stone of the sun
hovers like a golden fly
above the nether stone.
Everything is always.

"Sunt lacrimae rerum"

Things don't cry
but there are tears in them.
You open your handbag
and it's full of tears,
your wallet and lipstick
are floating, your keys
have sunk.
In the silver drawer
all the spoons are full of salt.
You leave the house
with tearstreaked windows
to walk on a huge,
angrily sobbing hill.
And the wind, the wind!

My Music

I will have music, I will, I will.
Music of drumming, the roar in the drum
that comes between the hitting sticks
constant and nowhere as lions in darkness.
I will have roaring. I will have singing
like green sap sticks in the stinging fire,
shrill, shrill, and sweet to kill,
I will have high loud singing, I will.
I will drum the roar till I break the drumhead.
I will sing shrill till the fire's dead.

A Painting

for Steve McLeod

The land lies dark as sleep is
between dreams: formless
matter of forms. Darkness
stretches on level beyond it
under the levels of a sky
dull jade green and grey.
And that is all there is. Except
a little above the middle, one
bright, far line of light on water.

Semen

Semen is soft stuff
made of little wrigglers,
silvery shoal–milk
with a smell of plum blossom,
reeking innocence.

Sometimes I see people,
even gangs and soldiers,
as small and vulnerable
polliwogs, schools
of minnows, skin–petals.

Seeing a half truth,
better not blink. Only
a moment and bingo
the heavy metal boot's in
and my one–eyed belly
hard with something huge.

The Red Dancers

for Lucille Clifton

The first time those dancers came to my town
I was scared, I cried, I wouldn't come out.
They went away yelling,
whirling red banners.
But they'd come back, four or five of them,
every so often, those girls,
so shameless that I was ashamed
to dance with them, so proud
that I was proud to learn
their difficult, painful dances.

The first time they didn't come
the people of my town
stood at the ends of streets
crying, "Where are you?"
till the moon turned blue.
And they came back,
yelling and laughing,
hurting and whirling.

They came too often, they danced too long.
The gutters of the streets ran red.
The people of my town
shut the gates against the dancers.
A long time now
since they stopped coming.
Nobody stands any more
waiting at the ends of streets.
Nobody whirls long red banners.

But I remember
all the steps of the dances.

Ariadne Dreams

The beat of sleep is all my mind.
I am my rhyme. I wind the ball
deeper and deeper in the maze
to find the meeting of the ways,
to find before the hero finds
the prisoner of the Labyrinth,
the horn-crowned horror at the end
of all the corridors, my friend.
I lead him forth. He kneels to graze
where grass grows thick above the tomb
and the light moves among the days.
The hero finds an empty room.
I seek my rhyme. I dance my will,
vaulting the wide horns of the bull.
The waves beat. What woman weeps
on the far seacoast of my sleep?

Waking: Two Poems

I

Drifting on the April river
of the dark, sweet winds
broken by birdsong rapids,
I am borne to daylight.

II

In the grey cocoon of light the mind
finds metamorphosis,
makes from the wreck of what she was
the wings of what she is.

Getting On

I that am love
this body that is
not for much longer.
We are old
partners in the sunlight
trade and fly by night
deals. We do collaborate
in getting on.

To the Next Guests

I have dreamed strange dreams
in this bed where you sleep
and may dream them.
Do not be afraid.
The transformation changes.
The ship will land.
You are not dead.

In this white-sailed bed
other strangers have slept.
A few of them I know of.
Most are undreamt of.
Maybe my dreams
were their dreams left
behind. The maid changes
the bed between guests.
No one is dead.

A Discourse on Method

If I puzzle you
I puzzle me: that palm
opens where to proffer
what blinding bearing?
Mind's end indeed: eyes
dazzle, mined to the dry end.
Smelt rather river ore, quick silver,
witch hazel, willow thickets,
not flat palm, and the back of my hand
to all that pomp and shivery.

What I Have

I have walked in the long rooms
of the house of the red sunsets
and broken the bread of my breath
at the board of the violent sea.

I have seen a doomed hawk in a high tree
mobbed by shouting crows and gulls
look into silence, silent,
being hawk being hawk only till death.

The Hard Dancing

Dancing on the sun is hard,
it burns your feet, you have to leap
higher and higher into the dark,
until you somersault to sleep.
The mountains of the sun are steep,
rising to shadow at the crown,
the valleys of the sun are deep
and ever brighter deeper down.